The Buddy Files

THE CASE OF THE
LST
BOY

Dori Hillestad Butler

Pictures by Jeremy Tugeau

Albert Whitman & Company
Chicago, Illinois

Library of Congress Cataloging-in-Publication Data

Butler, Dori Hillestad.

The Buddy files : the case of the lost boy / by Dori Hillestad Butler.

p. cm.

Summary: While searching for his mysteriously lost human family, Buddy the
dog is adopted by another family and helps solve the mystery of their missing boy.

ISBN 978-0-8075-0910-4
ISBN 978-0-8075-0932-6
[1. Dogs—Fiction. 2. Missing children—Fiction. 3. Mystery and detective stories.]
I. Title. II. Title: The case of the lost boy.

PZ7.B9759Bu 2010

[Fic]—dc22

2009023763

Text copyright © 2010 by Dori Hillestad Butler.

Illustrations copyright © 2010 by Jeremy Tugeau.

Published in 2010 by Albert Whitman & Company.

Printed in the U.S.A.

10 9 8 7 LB 15 14 13 12

The design is by Nick Tiemersma.

For more information about Albert Whitman & Company,
please visit our web site at www.albertwhitman.com.

For Bob, who has always given me
everything I needed to write.

Table of Contents

1
The P-O-U-N-D

Hello!

My name is King. I'm a dog.

I'm also a detective. I solve mysteries here in Four Lakes, Minnesota, with my human, Kayla.

Right now I have a mystery to solve by myself. It's about Kayla and her family.

I know where Kayla's mom is. She is in a place called the National Guard. That means she's far away.

Kayla and Dad aren't worried about her, so I'm not worried about her, either.

The people I'm worried about are Kayla and Dad. They've gone missing! It's up to me to find them.

"I have news for you, King," says Sam. Sam is a basset hound. He's locked inside the cage next door.

"Your people aren't missing. They just don't want you anymore. That's why they left you here."

"Here" is the **P-o-U-N-D**. We don't say it. We spell it. Sam doesn't know what he's talking about. "My people didn't leave me here," I say. "They would *never* leave me here.

9

They left me at Barker Bob's."

Barker Bob's is where I go for vacation. They have a big yard and a pool, and everyone is very relaxed. It's nothing like the **P-o-U-N-D**.

"My people said they were coming back," I tell Sam.

"They all say they're coming back," George mutters from the cage across from mine. George is an old bulldog. He is probably the oldest dog I've ever met.

"If my people say they're coming back, then they're coming back," I say.

But my people have been gone a long time. A *very* long time.

They've been gone so long that the alpha human at Barker Bob's said I couldn't stay there anymore. She called my neighbor, Mr. Sanchez, and he came and got me.

I stayed at the Sanchezes' house for eleventy-three days. But then Kayla's Uncle Marty came. I thought Uncle Marty was going to take me home, but he put me in his car. He unbuckled my collar and tossed it in the back seat. Then he drove me to the **P-o-U-N-D**. He told the people here that I did not have a home. And then he left.

I have never been crazy about Uncle Marty.

When you are at the **P-o-U-N-D**, you're supposed to choose new people.

I don't want *new* people; I want my old people.

But dogs who don't choose new people disappear from the **P-o-U-N-D.** Poof! Just like that. They are never seen or heard from again.

That's what happened to Ginger... and Kiki... and just yesterday, Oliver.

I would like to find out what happened to those dogs, but first I have to find out what happened to my people.

If you want to solve a mystery, you should start by making some lists. That's what Kayla and I did when we solved the Case of the Lost Frisbee, the Case of the Strange Footprints, and the Case of the Ghostly Presence.

Kayla wrote her lists in her detective's notebook. I kept my lists inside my head.

First we made a list of all the things we already knew about our case.

Here is what I know about the Case of the Missing Family:

🐾 My people's names are Kayla, Mom, and Dad.

🐾 Kayla and Dad were last seen in the lobby of Barker Bob's.

🐾 Mom is not missing.

🐾 Kayla and Dad said they were going to visit Grandma in Springtown. They said they would come back in one week.

🐾 Kayla and Dad never came back.

The second list Kayla and I made

when we solved a mystery was a list of things we didn't know.

Here is what I don't know about the Case of the Missing Family:

- 🐾 Did Kayla and Dad ever arrive at Grandma's house?
- 🐾 How long is one week?
- 🐾 Did Kayla and Dad ever leave Grandma's house?
- 🐾 Do Kayla and Dad know that I am at the P-o-U-N-D?
- 🐾 Where are Kayla and Dad?
- 🐾 Does Mom know that Kayla and Dad are missing?

The third list Kayla and I made was a list of things we were going to do to find out what we didn't know.

We called this the Plan.

Here is my plan right now:

- 🐾 Escape from the P-o-U-N-D.
- 🐾 Go back to my house and look for clues.
- 🐾 Find Grandma's house.
- 🐾 Find Kayla and Dad.

I am stuck at Escape from the P-o-U-N-D. How can I escape when I'm locked in this cage?

While I am thinking about this, a human boy and his mother come to visit. They stop in front of me.

"What do you think of this dog, Connor?" the human mother asks the human boy. I bet her name is Mom, too.

The boy doesn't look at me. And

he doesn't answer his mother. His
arms are folded tight across his chest.
He smells sad.

I wonder why he is so sad. I haul
myself up onto my legs and go over
to the mother and the boy. I sniff the
mother's shoes. They smell like new
carpet, pizza, a sweaty gym, other
dogs, and ... *Mole?* Not just any mole ...
this mother's shoes smell like the mole
I keep chasing out of Kayla's backyard.

I look up at the mother, and she
scratches my ears through the bars.
Actually, it's not just Mole that I smell
on this lady. If I take in a deep breath,
I can smell my whole neighborhood:
the Gormans' cat, the Sanchezes' plum
tree, flowers, bushes, humans, and
animals I know.

*Why does this stranger smell like
my neighborhood?*

I sniff at the boy's shoes and up
his pant leg. I can smell my neighborhood on him, too.

"Excuse me?" the mother says to
the guy who cleans our cages every
morning. We call him Hose Guy
because he always carries a hose
over his shoulder.

"Could we see this dog, please?"
the mother asks Hose Guy.

Hose Guy comes over and unlocks
my cage. He snaps a leash to my collar
and hands it to the mother. I sniff her
all over.

"Down, boy," Hose Guy says,
pulling me off the mother.

Oops. Humans don't like it when

you put your paws on them. But I can't help it. I love the smell of my neighborhood!

We all walk to the meet-and-greet room. I've never been here before. But I've heard about it. This is where they bring you to meet new families. Families you can adopt.

I've also heard that sometimes there are treats hidden around the meet-and-greet room. I press my nose to the ground and search for goodies.

Jackpot! There are dog biscuit crumbs under a chair. And one...

two... nine... five... THREE Cheerios. I LOVE Cheerios. They're my favorite food!

"I'm going to be the new principal at Four Lakes Elementary," the mother tells Hose Guy. "I'm starting in just a few weeks, and I'm looking for a dog that I can bring to school every day. It's good to have a dog around a school."

"This guy would make a fine dog for a school," Hose Guy says. "He's very calm and laid back for a golden retriever."

What do you mean "for a golden retriever?" We are all calm and laid back!

"He's also completely housebroken," Hose Guy says.

I don't know what that means.

But the mother does. And whatever it is, it makes her happy.

I want to make her happy because she smells like my neighborhood. Maybe she knows my humans. Maybe she can help me find them.

That's why when she asks me to sit, I sit. When she asks me to lie down, I lie down. And when she asks me to shake, I hold up my paw.

Now she is extra-happy. She is so happy that she turns to the boy and says, "What do you think, Connor? Should we adopt this fella?"

Wait a minute! Humans do not adopt dogs. Dogs adopt humans!

The boy, Connor, must know this because he does not answer his mother. He just hangs back by the corner.

He smells even sadder than he

smelled before. I go over to him and lick his hand because it's not his fault I can't adopt him. He and his mother are the kind of humans I would adopt if I didn't already have a family.

"We'll take him," the mother tells Hose Guy.

"What? No, you can't take me... I already have a family. Didn't you know? A DOG CAN ONLY HAVE ONE FAMILY!!!" I say this extra loud because it's important.

"I think he knows we're adopting him," Mom says. "Look how happy he is."

"HAPPY? YOU CALL THIS HAPPY?"

Everything happens really fast

after that. The alpha human at the **P-o-U-N-D** comes in and gives Mom some papers to write on. He gives me a new collar and Mom and Connor a new leash. Then they take me out of the meet-and-greet room ... down the hall ... and out to the parking lot. They don't even let me say goodbye to all my new friends.

But then it hits me: I have just escaped from the **P-o-U-N-D**!

And I wasn't even trying to.

Maybe adopting these people is not such a bad idea. I have crossed off this part of my plan: Escape from the **P-o-U-N-D**. Now I am one step closer to finding Kayla and Dad.

2
My Name Is King

"What's the matter, honey?" Mom asks the boy on the way to their house.

I am in the back seat, and they are in the front. I spot a French fry on the floor. I LOVE French fries. They're my favorite food!

"I thought you wanted a dog," Mom says.

"I just want to go home," Connor grumbles. "Back to our *real* house in California."

Mom grips the steering wheel extra-tight. "I know you miss your dad and your friends," she says. "But we're going to be happy here in Minnesota, Connor. You'll see. Your dad and I will watch for sales on airplane tickets. We'll send you back to California for a visit as often as we can afford to."

Connor stares out the window. I don't know where California is, but it must be far away if you have to fly there in an airplane. Connor must miss his dad as much as I miss Kayla. I put my paws up on his seat and lick his ear to show him I understand.

Mom pushes me down. "You stay in the backseat, boy," she says.

"I will," I tell her with my eyes. But she is driving, so she doesn't notice. She probably wouldn't understand even if she did notice. Most humans her age don't understand Dog at all.

"We need to come up with a name for him," Mom tells Connor.

I already have a name. But Mom and Connor don't know that.

"What do you think of Buddy?" Mom asks.

Buddy? That's a wimp's name! My name is King. K-I-N-G. I am the King of Crime-solving. That's what Kayla says. And she is my queen.

"Don't you think Buddy is a good name for a dog that's going to go to school?" Mom asks. "We want him to be everyone's buddy."

I put my paws back up on the front seat. "Tell her no," I say to Connor. "Tell her you want to call me 'King.'"

Connor shrugs. "Whatever," he says. Then he turns around and looks at me. I think he wants to pet me.

"Go ahead," I tell him. I stretch my neck closer to him. "You can pet me."

But he just sits there. I can't tell whether he understands me or not.

We drive a little farther, and then my nose starts to twitch. Something smells familiar.

I can see it through the front window. *It's the park!* The park where Kayla takes me to play detective. You'd be surprised how many mysteries there are to solve in a park.

I stare out the side window. I check out the kids who are playing ball…and the kids who are playing on the climbing toy…and the kid who is reading on the bench.

None of them is Kayla.

Mom turns at the corner. We are close to my house. *Very* close.

Mom pulls into a driveway, and I am going crazy inside myself. Kayla, the other Mom, and Dad live in the Carrs' old house, just behind this one. What luck! I can to go back to my house and look for clues.

"Look," Mom says as she opens

the door for me. "He knows this is his house already."

No. My house is the one behind *this one.*

Now I know why I smelled my neighborhood on Connor and Mom. They *live* in my neighborhood. I can tell they haven't lived here very long, though. There are boxes piled everywhere. I sniff at a couple of them. Laundry soap. Electric stuff. And ... something else I can't quite make out.

"Are you hungry, Buddy?" Mom asks. She shakes some dry food into a bowl.

Oh, boy! FOOD!!!

And it's good food, too. Big colorful pellets. A blend of wonderful things like chicken, fish, and liver. Much better than those little brown pellets they had at Barker Bob's. And way better than the mushy stuff at the **P-o-U-N-D**.

They also have a nice big bed for me. Oops. Maybe not.

Mom grabs me by my brand-new collar and pulls me off the bed. "No dogs on the furniture!"

But wait! They have another bed for me. It's in Connor's room, and it's just my size. I can reach it without jumping. Mom points to it and says, "Lie down."

I lie down. This bed is like Kayla's pillow except it's for my whole body, not just my head.

They also have a really cool bird toy. It's soft and squishy. You can tug it. You can carry it around. You can even make it squeak. I think I could live here...if I didn't already have a family.

Mom leaves Connor and me alone. As soon as she's gone, Connor gets down on the floor and starts petting me. Ha! I knew he wanted to pet me. He's very good at it, too. He doesn't just rub my head a little bit like some humans do. He runs his hand down my whole back. Mmm. Heaven. He must really like me.

Hey, I wonder if he likes me enough to let me be on his bed when his mom isn't looking? I hop up. He

does not push me off.

I can see out his window from here. I can see over the tall wood fence into my backyard. I see the big tree where I chase the squirrels. I see Kayla's swing set. I see my house. There are no lights on inside.

Connor plops down on the bed beside me. He wraps his arms around me and buries his head in my fur. Kayla used to do that.

"It's not that I don't want you, Buddy," he says.

"*King*," I tell him. "My name is King."

Connor sits back up. "I used to want a dog really bad. But my dad is allergic to dogs so we couldn't ever have one."

I've heard of dogs who are allergic to people, but I never knew people could be allergic to dogs.

"But my mom and dad just got divorced," Connor goes on. "So now we can have a dog. My mom says she wants you for school, but I know she really got you for me. To make up for having to move so far away from Dad and all my friends."

I'm not sure anything can make up for having to leave part of your family.

"The thing is..." Connor leans closer to me. "This might be Mom's new home, but it isn't mine. I'll probably go back to California someday. And I won't be able to take you with me."

3
Stranger Danger

Connor lets me sleep in his bed
with him all night long. What Mom
doesn't know won't hurt her.

The next morning, Mom pours
some more of that yummy food into
a bowl and sets it on the floor for
me. Then Connor slips me pieces
of bacon under the table. Mmm!
I LOVE bacon. It's my favorite food!

After breakfast, Mom says,

"Connor? Please take Buddy for a walk."

I sit up. Walk? I LOVE walks. They're my favorite thing!

"Okay. In a minute," Connor says. He gets up from the table and goes to his room.

I follow him. "We *are* going for a walk, aren't we?" I ask him with my eyes.

He doesn't answer. He grabs some papers and coins from the top of his dresser and stuffs them in his pocket.

Papers and coins! When Kayla brings papers and coins on our walks, we stop for ice cream. I LOVE ice cream. It's my favorite food!

We go back out to the kitchen and Connor snaps the leash to my collar.

Then we are on our way.

Oh, boy! Birds. Squirrels. Rabbits. Fresh air.

"Slow down, boy," Connor says, tugging on my leash.

Oops. I forget that humans can't walk as fast as dogs.

I try to walk slower. I try to walk right next to Connor. Humans like it when you walk right next to them.

"KING?" I hear a loud, familiar voice. "KING, IS IT REALLY YOU?"

"Mouse!" I cry. Mouse is my friend—my best friend who is not human. He lives two houses down from Connor.

"Slow down, Buddy!" Connor says again.

But I am so excited to see Mouse

that I can't slow down. Maybe Mouse knows what happened to my people?

"WHERE HAVE YOU BEEN?" Mouse yells even though I am standing right in front of him. He can't help yelling. He is just a loud dog. He is the biggest, loudest dog on our block.

It's been so long since we've seen each other that we are sniffing each other like crazy through the fence.

"WHERE'S KAYLA?" Mouse asks. "AND WHO'S THAT KID WITH YOU?"

"This is Connor," I tell Mouse.

There's something that happens to humans when they get scared. They look different. They sound different. They *smell* different. It's

hard to describe unless you're a dog.
But trust me. My new friend Connor
is scared to death of my old friend
Mouse.

Lots of humans are scared of
Mouse. It's weird because Mouse
is probably the friendliest dog
on the whole block. I don't
think he would
even hurt
a flea.

"Hi, Connor," Mouse says in a voice that is soft for Mouse, but still pretty loud.

Connor backs away. "Let's go, Buddy," he says, yanking on my collar.

"BUDDY?" Mouse says as Connor drags me away. "DID THAT KID JUST CALL YOU BUDDY?"

"It's a long story," I tell him over my shoulder. "Hey, have you seen my people?"

"NO!" Mouse says. "I'VE BEEN ASKING AROUND. NO ONE HAS SEEN YOU OR YOUR PEOPLE IN A LONG TIME. I WAS GETTING WORRIED."

I'm still worried. I wish I could stay and chat, but Connor is in a big hurry to get away from Mouse.

"Okay, okay, I'm coming," I tell
Connor.

Connor tries to cross the street,
but I pull him back.

"Let's go this way instead," I say.

I'm happy that Connor follows
me. This is the way to Kayla's house.
All we have to do is keep going
straight until we get to the corner.
Then we turn … and we turn again
at the next corner … and pretty soon
we'll be there! Then maybe we can
search for clues. Searching for clues
is another part of my plan.

It's been a long time since I last
walked through my neighborhood.
I can smell a fresh rabbit hole in

the Tuckers' yard. I want to check it out, but my collar tightens as Connor pulls me back. I guess I will have to check it out later.

Oh, no. Did the Gormans get another cat?

We turn the corner. Who is this guy walking toward us? I have never seen him before. I don't think he lives around here.

I don't like the way he is looking at us. And I really don't like the way he smells. He smells...*dangerous.*

"Hello," he says to Connor.

I keep walking. I don't want Connor to talk to this man.

But Connor stops and says hello anyway.

I don't understand why Connor is

afraid of Mouse, but he's not afraid of this man. Can't he smell the danger?

"Nice dog," the man says through his teeth.

He's lying. He doesn't think I'm a nice dog at all. He wants to hurt me. He wants to hurt Connor. I can't explain how I know this. I just do. Just like I know when a human is happy, sad, mad, or scared. It's a skill most dogs have.

I growl at the man to warn him he'd better leave me and Connor alone.

"Buddy!" Connor says, like I did a bad thing.

But the growling works. The man takes two steps back, and Connor and I continue on our way.

The man is still watching us, though.

Is he going to follow us?

I hope not. I keep checking over my shoulder, but I don't see him coming. What a relief.

Connor and I keep going. We turn another corner, and I forget all about that man because we're on *my* street now. My house is straight ahead.

I can smell it. I can see it. I run toward it as fast as I can. As fast as Connor can run.

There are newspapers in the driveway. Lots of newspapers. I sniff the entire pile. Interesting. Some of them weren't delivered by our regular paper girl.

I sniff all around the driveway.

I sniff the grass. I sniff the big tree
in the middle of the yard. Other dogs
have been here. Dogs I don't know.

"What are you doing, Buddy?"
Connor asks as he follows me around
my yard.

"Looking for clues," I tell him.

The only clue I have found so far
is: My people haven't been here in
a very long time. I can hardly smell
them at all. And this is their yard.

I think Connor understands what
I said because he lets go of my leash.
Good! It's much easier to search for
clues when you aren't dragging a
human behind you.

I scamper up the front steps. I peer
inside the tall, skinny window next to
the door. There are no lights on inside.

45

No jackets on the hook. No shoes by the door.

Something is wrong. I can feel it all the way from my head to my tail. If only I could go inside and check things out. I try and wiggle the door open with my nose. It doesn't budge.

I scratch at the door. But no one comes to let me in.

There's a window on the back porch that's sometimes open. Maybe I can get in through there?

I race around the side of the house, but the gate is closed. I can't get to the backyard.

I check the other side of the house. This gate is closed, too. What now?

Maybe Connor will open the gate

for me. I go back around to the front
of the house.

But when I get there, Connor is
gone.

4
Nose to the Ground

Where's Connor?

I peer up and down the street. I don't see him anywhere.

What happened? Where'd he go?

I see a pair of squinty eyes in the bushes across the street. They're too low to the ground to be Connor's eyes. Too yellow, too.

I know who it is. It's Cat with No Name.

Cat with No Name and I are not friends. But maybe he saw something. Maybe he knows where Connor went.

"Did you see me with a boy a little while ago?" I call to the cat.

"Of course," he replies. He blinks his eyes. "I'm not blind."

Cats can be rude sometimes, but I try not to let it get to me.

"Did you see where the boy went?" I ask.

The cat steps out from the bushes. "Yes."

I wait for him to say more, but he just licks his paw.

"Where did he go?" I ask.

"Away."

"Away where?"

"How would I know? Is it my job to

keep track of all your humans?"

Connor isn't exactly *my* human, but that's beside the point. "What exactly did you see?" I ask.

"I told you," the cat says. "I saw you with the human. I saw you run around to the backyard. I saw the human run away."

Connor ran away? "Where did he go?"

The cat sighs. "Don't you listen? I've just told you twice now. He ran *away*."

Cats aren't just rude. They're also not very helpful.

"Thanks," I say. Thanks for nothing. I turn around and press my nose to the ground. I'll find Connor by myself. It hasn't been that long

since he was here. It shouldn't be hard
to pick up his scent.

Ah. There it is. A sweet blending
of bacon, eggs, toothpaste, and dirt.
Connor.

I follow the trail. Around the
tree ... across the yard ... down the
sidewalk ... out into the street ... and ...
that's it.

The scent is gone. Just like that.
Right here in the middle of the street.

Where did he go? I can't tell.
There are too many smells: humans,
flowers, squirrels, rabbits, cars,
trucks, buses.

A poodle and his human walk
toward me. I don't think they live
around here. I've never seen them
before.

"What are you looking for?" the poodle asks.

"I'm looking for a boy that smells like bacon, eggs, toothpaste, and dirt. Have you smelled him? Have you seen him?"

"I don't think so," the poodle says. "Where did you lose him?"

"Right here."

The poodle's human picks up my leash. He smells like peanut butter. I LOVE peanut butter. It's my favorite food!

"Did you get away from someone, boy?" Peanut Butter Human asks me. "Do you have a tag?" He feels along my collar, but there is no tag. Not anymore.

Uh-oh. No tag. No human. If I'm

not careful, I'm going to end up right back at the **P-O-U-N-D**.

I have to get out of here. I jerk my collar out of the human's grasp and RUN.

"Wait!" Peanut Butter Human calls after me. "Come back!"

But no way am I going back. I run, run, run ... as fast as I can. I don't even look over my shoulder until I am around the corner.

Whew! Peanut Butter Human is not following me.

I round another corner, and I'm back on Connor's street. My nose twitches. I pick up Connor's trail, but I think it's the trail he left when he was with me. I don't think he's been back.

Mouse lifts his head when I pass by his house. "HEY, KING," he says. "WHAT'S THE MATTER? YOU SMELL WORRIED."

I explain how I have lost another human. And this one doesn't even belong to me. I feel like I am losing humans left and right.

"OH, COME ON," Mouse says. "THE BOY MAY NOT ACTUALLY BE LOST. MAYBE HE FOUND HIS WAY HOME."

"How?" I wonder. "How could he have gotten home ahead of me? And if he went home, why does his trail lead to the middle of the road and then disappear?"

"MAYBE SOMEONE IN A CAR PICKED HIM UP AND TOOK HIM

HOME," Mouse says.

"Maybe," I say. "But who would do that? The family just moved here. They don't know many people."

"WOULD HE GET INTO A CAR WITH A STRANGER?" Mouse asks.

I gulp. I hope not. Bad things can happen if you get into a car with someone you don't know.

"TELL YOU WHAT," Mouse says. "WHY DON'T YOU GO HOME AND SEE IF HE'S THERE? I'LL PUT OUT AN ALERT OVER THE NETWORK AND SEE WHAT I CAN FIND OUT."

Mouse is the perfect dog to send out an alert. He's so loud that dogs several blocks away can hear him.

Those dogs will pass the message

on to other dogs. Pretty soon the whole town will know we're looking for Connor.

"Thanks, Mouse."

I continue on to Connor's house. My nose is in overdrive. I smell Connor here and I smell him there, but I can't tell if these are new smells or old smells.

When I get back to the house, I scratch on the front door. Mom opens it.

"Buddy!" she exclaims. She looks around. "Where's Connor?"

My tail droops. "You mean he's not here?"

Mom comes all the way out of the house. She picks up my leash, then peers up and down the street.

"Where's Connor?" she asks again. Louder this time.

I can't even look at her. "I don't know," I mumble.

It's my fault he's lost. I should have been watching him. I should have stayed with him. But instead I went searching for clues about my family.

I'm a *bad dog.*

Mom leads me inside. "You stay here," she says. She doesn't even unsnap my leash. She heads back outside and closes the door behind her.

Hey! What about me? I scratch at the door. *Don't you want me to help you find Connor?*

But I am talking to a closed door.

I run to the window. Mom is already halfway up the block. I hear her calling, "Connor! Connor, where are you?"

"Please," I howl. "Come back and get me! I can help you find him!"

Mom keeps walking. I don't think her hearing is very good.

"YOU'RE NOT EVEN HEADING IN THE RIGHT DIRECTION," I yell.

It doesn't matter. Mom continues up the hill until I don't see her anymore.

5
Jelly Donut and Plain Donut

Mom is gone a long time. A really long time. I wonder if she's ever coming back.

I climb up onto the couch because sometimes that makes humans come back faster. But it doesn't seem to work this time.

I go to the front door. Too bad it's not a door like the garage door at Kayla's house. To open that door, all you have to do is jump really high and hit the button with your nose. But you need human paws to open this kind of door. You need to be able to wrap your whole paw around it, turn it, and pull. All at the same time. I've never met a dog who could do it.

I walk around and check all the doors and windows in the whole house. Just in case there is one that is open.

There isn't.

I go back to the couch and wait. And wait.

And wait some more.

Finally Mom comes back. She is alone.

I hop down from the couch and go to greet her at the door.

She doesn't pay any attention to me. She goes straight to the kitchen and picks up the phone.

"Hello? My son is missing," she says into the phone. "About an hour... but he's only nine! Yes... yes... okay, thank you."

She hangs up and starts walking back and forth inside the house. I don't know why she does this. She's not going to find Connor *inside* the house. If she wants to find him, we have to go back outside.

The doorbell rings, and Mom and I hurry to the door. There are two police officers standing on the front step. Mom opens the door to let them in, and I think about running out to go look for Connor some more. But it's

probably better to stay here and see
if I can help the police.

Besides, they smell good. I can
tell that one of them had a jelly-filled
donut for breakfast. He's even got
a small blob of jelly on his pants. I
lick it up and he pats my head. The
other officer had a plain donut for
breakfast.

I am not picky about my donuts.
Plain donuts. Jelly-filled donuts.
Donuts with sprinkles. They're all
my favorite food!

Jelly Donut takes out a notebook
and a pen. "I understand your boy is
missing?" he says.

"Yes," Mom says. Her voice cracks.
"He took our dog for a walk. The dog
came back, but he didn't. I don't know

where he could be."

"Don't worry, Ma'am," Plain Donut says. "We'll find him. But first we need to ask you some questions. When did you last see him? What time?"

"About eight-thirty this morning."

"And what time did the dog come back?" Jelly Donut asks.

I'm not sure what time is, but humans sure talk about it a lot.

"It was ten after nine," Mom says. "He's a new dog. We just got him yesterday. I don't know if he pulled too hard and Connor couldn't hold onto his leash or ... if something happened."

She means something bad.

Could something bad have happened to Connor?

While Mom and the police talk

some more, I make a list inside my head of all the bad things that could have happened to Connor:

🐾 He could have gotten hurt.

🐾 He could have run away. He could have gone back to where his dad and his friends live.

🐾 He could have been kidnapped!

I know all about kidnapping. That's when a stranger—or sometimes not a stranger—takes you away from your house or your neighborhood and something bad happens. That's what Uncle Marty did to me when he took me to the P-o-U-N-D.

Next I try and think of reasons why none of these things could have happened to Connor.

Here's why Connor couldn't have gotten hurt:

If Connor were hurt, I would have found him.

Unless a human stopped to help him. Maybe that human had a car. Maybe the human took him to the hospital. That would explain why Connor's trail disappeared in the middle of the street.

But if he was at the hospital, wouldn't someone have called Mom?

Here's why Connor couldn't have run away:

He hasn't lived here very long. He doesn't have anyone to run away to. Not in Four Lakes.

He might try to go back to where

his dad and his friends live. But they live in place called California.

It would be hard for Connor to go back there.

California is so far away that Connor would have to drive eleventy-three days to get there. Connor is too young to drive. Or he would have to take an airplane. But there are no airplanes on our block.

Here's why Connor couldn't have been kidnapped:

I don't want to even think about Connor being kidnapped.

But Kayla says a good detective thinks about every possibility. Even the possibilities he doesn't want to think about.

I think about that strange man we passed. The one who smelled dangerous. Could he be the kidnapping kind of dangerous? Could he have come back while I was sniffing around Kayla's house? Could he have come back with his car and taken Connor away?

The police ask Mom a few more questions. Unimportant things like what does Connor look like? He looks like any other boy. What is he wearing today? He is wearing a shirt and pants, like every other boy.

These are not questions that will help us find Connor. Here are some better questions to ask:

Can you describe Connor's scent?

Connor smells like bacon, eggs, toothpaste, and dirt.

Where was Connor last seen?

Open the door and I will take you there.

Have you noticed anything unusual in the neighborhood today? Anything that made you feel uncomfortable?

Yes. There was a strange man. He smelled dangerous. We saw him just before Connor disappeared. "Open the door and I will see if I can find him," I say to the police.

"Buddy!" Mom says sharply. "Stop barking!"

Barking. Such an ugly-sounding word. It means talking with your mouth rather than your eyes or your ears or your tail. Humans bark more than any other animal, yet they don't like it when anyone else does it.

"Do you know which direction he went with your dog?" Jelly Donut asks.

Mom gazes out the window. "I think they went that way." She points up the hill.

"No!" I say. "We went the other way. Open the door and I'll show you where we went. I'll show you where I was when I noticed Connor was gone. I'll show you where I picked up his trail, and I'll show you where it disappeared."

"Have you asked any of your neighbors whether they've seen him?"

Plain Donut asks Mom.

"Mouse put out an alert," I say.

It's like I'm invisible. No one pays any attention to me at all.

"We don't really know any of our neighbors yet," Mom says.

"Doesn't matter," Jelly Donut says. "Do you have a picture of your son? We'll knock on some doors and see if anyone has seen him."

Mom opens her purse and pulls out a picture of Connor. She hands it to Jelly Donut. Then they all head for the door.

As soon as the door opens, I hear Mouse calling out to me. "KING! KING! CAN YOU HEAR ME? I HAVE NEWS ABOUT YOUR BOY!"

6
Smells Like a Kidnapping

"News?" I cry. "What news?" I
hope I can get the news before the
door closes.

"BUSTER JUST TALKED TO
SOMEONE FROM THE NEXT
NEIGHBORHOOD OVER," I hear
Mouse call from down the street.
"IT SOUNDS LIKE YOUR HUMAN
MAY BE PLAYING AT THE PARK."

"He's there now?" I wiggle my
nose in between the door and Jelly
Donut's leg and squeeze my way out.

I have to get to the park. I have
to find Connor.

"Buddy!" Mom yells at me. "Come
back here!"

"I know where Connor is," I call
back to her. "Follow me!"

I keep on running. I dart
through the Deerbergs' backyard...
through the flowers...through the
Sanchezes' backyard.

I run all the way to the park.
It feels strange to be here without
Kayla. But I can't think about Kayla
right now. I have to think about
Connor. Where *is* he?

I check the swings. I check the

climbing toy. I check inside the slide.

No Connor.

I check the bushes. I check the other bushes. I check the creek.

Still no Connor.

I put my nose to the ground and sniff. I sniff all around the park, but I don't pick up Connor's scent anywhere.

"Hey!" I call out to anyone who can hear me. "I'm the one who is looking for the missing boy. My friend Mouse heard through the Network that my boy was at the park. Did someone smell him there?

Several nearby dogs start talking at once:

"I smelled him!"

"I smelled him, too!"

"Toast, cereal, soap, and sweaty socks, right? You'll pick up his scent over by the swings."

Toast, cereal, soap, and sweaty socks? No, that's not Connor.

"Connor smells like eggs, bacon, toothpaste, and dirt," I say.

Silence.

"Sounds like the message got a little mixed up," says a little dog across the street.

That happens sometimes. One dog mixes up the information a little bit. The next dog mixes it up more. Pretty soon the message is completely wrong.

My shoulders sag. "So none of you has smelled a mix of eggs, bacon, toothpaste, and dirt?"

"No." "Nope." "Sorry," they all reply.

If I were human, I could let the sadness and frustration I'm feeling drip out of my eyes. Since I'm not human, I have no choice but to carry the sadness and frustration in my heart.

"We'll send out another alert," says a big dog from a block away.

I hear the alert go out: "Please report back to Mouse or King if you smell eggs, bacon, toothpaste, and dirt."

But Connor could be anywhere by now.

While I am standing there trying to decide what to do next, a couple of police officers come up behind me. These are not the same donut-eating

police officers who were at Connor's
house a little while ago.

One is a lady police officer who
smells like burnt toast. I am not a
fan of burnt toast, but I will eat it
if it's there. The other officer smells
like a fishing boat.

"There he is!" Burnt Toast Lady
says.

"Grab him," Fishing Boat says.

Grab who? Me?

I take off running again. No one
else has done much to find Connor.
It's up to me.

"Somebody! Grab that dog!"
Fishing Boat calls out.

And before I know it, all the
humans in the entire park are
chasing me.

I leap over a swing … duck under the climbing toy … and RUN.

All the way to the fence.

Uh-oh. Dead end. There is nowhere to run.

Burnt Toast Lady snaps a leash to my collar. Fishing Boat talks into a small box. "We've got the dog," he says. "Where should we take him?"

I hear crackling inside that box. Then a voice: "Back to his house. 2120 Holiday Drive. The mother is waiting there." At least they aren't taking me back to the **P-o-U-N-D**.

The two police officers walk me back to Connor's house.

"We should come back and talk to people in the park," Burnt Toast Lady says to Fishing Boat. "Maybe someone has seen the missing boy."

"We should also search the park," Fishing Boat says. "Maybe he's hiding somewhere?"

"No, no," I tell them. "He's not in the park. I would have picked up his scent if he was."

We cross the street where Kayla lives.

"Let's go this way," I say, pulling on the leash. "I'll show you where I lost Connor."

"Wow, this is one strong dog," Burnt Toast Lady says. She tightens her grip on my leash.

I'm thinking she's pretty strong, too. She pulls me from Kayla's street and leads me to Connor's street.

"Hey, isn't this the neighborhood

where that guy tried to get some kid
to go into his car last week?" Fishing
Boat asks.

I gulp.

"Yes. It was a couple blocks from
here," Burnt Toast Lady says. "We
never did find the car."

"That kid got away, though,"
Fishing Boat says. "That's the
important thing."

"Do you think we're looking at
a kidnapping with this kid?" Burnt
Toast Lady asks.

"Nah," Fishing Boat replies. "I
think this is just a lost kid."

I hope so. Lost kids are usually
found. But kidnapped kids? I don't
want to think about it.

7
What Do I Know?

I'm depressed. The police brought
me back to Connor's house. Then
they went back to look for Connor
some more. Without me.

Without Mom, too. I think she's
as depressed as I am.

"I feel like I should be out looking
for Connor with everyone else," Mom
says as she stares out the window.

Me, too.

Mom turns to me. "Do you know where Connor is, Buddy?" she asks.

"No," I say. "I wish I did." I lick her hand because I feel bad that I don't know.

Mom lets out a breath of air. "I sure wish you could talk," she says, scratching my ears.

I can. I wish you could understand me.

"I bet you saw something when you were out with him," Mom says. "I bet you know something the rest of us don't know. I wish you could tell us what that is."

But I *didn't* see anything. And now I don't think I know anything that would help Mom or the police find Connor.

Here is what I know:

🐾 Connor and I left his house together.

🐾 He was still with me when we got to Kayla's house.

🐾 He disappeared when I tried to go into Kayla's backyard.

🐾 I followed Connor's scent around the yard and down the street.

🐾 Connor's scent disappeared in the middle of the street.

Here is what I don't know:

🐾 Where is Connor?

🐾 Why does his scent disappear
in the middle of the street?
🐾 Is he okay?

I don't have a plan to find out what
I don't know. And I don't know how to
make one.

I flop down on my belly and put
my head on my paws. Who am I
kidding? I'm not the King of Crime-
solving. I'm not even good at solving
mysteries. Not by myself. Kayla is the
one who is good at solving mysteries.
If Kayla was here, she'd know what
to do.

So ... what would Kayla do? I ask
myself.

"Huh?" I say. Because I don't
normally talk to myself.

But I ask again: *What would Kayla do?* How would she find Connor?

Kayla says we always know more than we think we do. The problem is we don't always *know* what we know.

I think about my lists. I think so hard I give myself a headache. Do I know more than I think I do?

Maybe...

I also know:

- 🐾 **Mouse put out an alert.**
- 🐾 **No dog has reported seeing Connor.**

What does that mean?

It means Connor disappeared when no dog was looking.

But a *cat* was looking. Maybe Cat with No Name knows more than he

85

thinks he does? Or maybe he knows more than he told me?

I could talk to Cat with No Name again.

What else do I know?

🐾 **Connor and I passed a stranger who smelled dangerous.**

🐾 **The police said that a stranger tried to get a kid into his car a couple blocks from here.**

I could also try to look for the stranger from this morning and see what I can find out about him.

Kayla would probably watch him and write down the things that he did in her notebook. If he went somewhere, she would follow him.

Kayla would also go back to the scene of the crime. Or in this case, back to the place where Connor disappeared. She would sit there for eleventy-five minutes and write down everything that happened. This is called a stakeout.

Unfortunately, a stakeout does not involve steak. I LOVE steak. It's my favorite food!

If I set up a stakeout where Connor disappeared, maybe I will see something that will help me solve this mystery.

Now I have several plans:

- 🐾 Talk to Cat with No Name.
- 🐾 Find the stranger from this morning and see what I can

learn about him.
* Set up a stakeout where
   Connor disappeared.

The only problem is I can't do any of these things from inside the house. I have to go out.

I walk over to Mom and let out a small woof.

Mom looks at me. "You want to go outside?"

Yes! I head for the door. But Mom doesn't follow.

"You've already been out twice this morning," Mom says in a tired voice. "You don't need to go out again."

"Yes, I do! If you want to find Connor, you have to let me outside."

Mom tilts her head at me. Does

she understand? "Do you *really* need to go outside again?" she asks.

"Yes! Yes, I do!" I wag my tail to show her how badly I need to go outside. Once I'm out, I'm going to go around the block and set up my stakeout. If I'm lucky, Cat with No Name and the stranger from this morning will walk by while I'm there.

"Well," Mom says. "I can't just sit here and do nothing. Maybe you and I should take a short walk."

"Well … okay. If you want to come along, that would be fine. Maybe you can write down what we see on the stakeout. Since your paws work better for writing than mine do."

"We're not going very far," Mom

warns me. "Just around the block. Maybe we'll get an idea of where Connor could have gone."

Around the block is exactly where we need to go.

Mom grabs my leash and snaps it to my collar. "Maybe we should think about putting in a doggy door," she mutters. "The backyard is fenced. If we had a doggy door, you could go in and out whenever you wanted."

"Really?" I say, wagging my tail. "You'd get me a doggy door? That would be SO COOL!"

I know other dogs who have doggy doors. But I've never had one myself. I've always wanted one.

Wait a minute. I won't be here

long enough to enjoy the doggy door if Mom puts one in. As soon as we find Connor, I'll have to start looking for my family again. And when I find them, I'll go back to my real home.

8
Smells Scary

Mom leads me down the front walk and turns toward the hill.

"No, not that way," I tell her. "We want to go this direction." I pull her away from the hill.

But as usual, Mom doesn't understand. And she's strong, so we end up going her way instead of mine. We'll still get to the place where Connor disappeared. We'll still be able to set

up a stakeout. It will just take us
longer to get there.

We pass Mr. Parker's house.
Mr. Parker is out raking his lawn.
Mr. Parker is *always* raking his
lawn. There are never any leaves
on it.

"Hello, there," Mr. Parker says to
Mom. My nose twitches. Something
about Mr. Parker's yard smells
strange today. A new person has
been here. It's somebody I've smelled
before, but I can't quite remember
where. It isn't a very nice smell,
though. Kind of sweaty and ... a little
bit *scary*.

"Hi," Mom says. "I'm Sarah
Keene. We just moved in down the
street."

Mr. Parker sets his rake against a tree and limps over to us. Mr. Parker has a bad leg, but that never stops him from working in his yard.

"Welcome to the neighborhood," he says to Mom.

"Thank you," Mom says. She takes out a picture and shows it to Mr. Parker. "My son was out walking the dog a little while ago, and the dog came back by himself. I'm afraid my son may have gotten lost. Have you seen this boy?"

Mr. Parker pulls a pair of glasses out of his pocket and rests them on the end of his nose. He peers at the picture.

"Can't say that I have. But my brother is visiting from Mankato.

He went out for a walk this morning.
Maybe he saw your boy."

I didn't know Mr. Parker had a
brother.

Mr. Parker turns toward his
house. "Jerry!" he calls. "Hey, Jerry!
Come out here a minute."

The door opens, and I can hardly
believe my eyes. The stranger from
this morning steps out of Mr. Parker's
house. He stiffens when he sees me.

"That's him!" I tell Mom. "That's
the stranger Connor and I saw this
morning."

"Buddy!" Mom says sharply.

"But, that's the guy!" I tell her,
tugging at my leash. "Can't you smell
him? Doesn't he smell dangerous?"
I think he smells like things that

jump out at you when you don't expect them. Now I know why Mr. Parker's yard smells funny.

"Jerry, this lady is looking for her son." Mr. Parker limps toward Jerry with the picture Mom handed him. "He was out walking with the dog—"

Jerry glances at the picture. "Yeah, I saw them."

"Where?" Mom asks. "How long ago?"

"Did you follow us around the corner?" I ask Jerry. "Did you ... *kidnap* Connor?" I can usually tell if a human is lying or if he's telling the truth.

I think Jerry knows this about me because he doesn't answer Mom or me. He starts to back away.

"You'll have to excuse my brother,"
Mr. Parker tells Mom. "He doesn't
like dogs very much."

Of course he doesn't. Because we
sense things that humans don't.

"I know you don't like me, Jerry,"
I say, pressing closer to him. "And
I don't much like you, either. I don't
like humans who—"

"I had a run-in with a dog a couple
weeks ago," Jerry tells Mom. He rolls
up his sleeve. His arm is covered with
bandages.

I stop and stare. I'm ... stunned.

"You mean ... a *dog* did that?" I ask.

I think Mom is a little surprised,
too. "I'm so sorry," she says. "Buddy
is a nice dog, though." She pats my
head to prove it. "He won't hurt you."

I don't know what to say. I sniff at Jerry again. He doesn't smell so scary anymore. He smells … *scared,* not scary. Sometimes it's hard to tell the difference between a human who is scary and a human who is scared. I think that's because sometimes the scariest humans are also scared of something.

Jerry is scared of *me.* That's why he watched us so closely. When he said "nice dog," he was probably telling me to BE a nice dog. Be a nice dog and don't hurt him.

Cross off another part of my plan to find Connor. I found the stranger from this morning—Jerry didn't have anything to do with Connor's disappearance.

Mr. Parker adjusts his glasses
and takes a good hard look at me.
"Say, have you met the Dixons yet?"
Mr. Parker asks Mom.

My tail stands straight up. *The
Dixons? Those are my people!* Kayla,
Mom, and Dad.

"No, not yet," Mom says. "Where
do they live?"

"On the next street over," Mr.
Parker says. "They have a dog that
looks just like yours."

"Really?" Mom says.

"'Course, I haven't seen that dog
around lately," Mr. Parker says. "The
lady is in the military, and I think
the dad and little girl went out of
town a while back. They probably
took the dog with them."

I wish.

"I'll look forward to meeting them," Mom says. "Goodbye."

Then we start walking again.

Now I am on the lookout for Cat with No Name and for a place to set up our stakeout.

We continue down the street, around the corner … and around another corner. We're getting close to Kayla's house. But we're coming at it from a different direction. As we get close, I pick up Connor's scent again. I follow it VERY carefully … zigzagging across the sidewalk and the grass … just in case I missed a clue before.

"What are you doing, Buddy?" Mom asks.

"Looking for Connor," I tell her.
She has a short memory. Isn't that
why we're on this walk? So that we
can set up a stakeout and find
Connor?

I follow Connor's scent across
the grass and out toward the street.
There is a sharp tug on my collar.

"No, Buddy," Mom says. "We're
not going to cross the street."

"But we have to," I tell her.
"That's where Connor disappeared."

I pull harder and Mom grabs
the leash with both hands. She is
stronger than she looks.

"I think we need to sign up for
an obedience class," she says, holding
tight to my leash. "I'm not going to
be able to take you to school unless I

can control you better."

I don't know what obedience is, but I'm not going to worry about that now. We have to find Connor!

I look both ways, then pull hard on my leash one more time. Sniff... sniff... sniff... I follow Connor's scent to the place where it ends.

"Buddy," Mom says. "Let's get out of the street."

"In a minute," I tell her. "We can set up our stakeout over by that tree. But first I want to make sure I didn't miss any clues."

I sniff. I listen. I look.

Up ahead a bus wheezes to a stop next to the curb. I stand there and watch as three humans get off the bus and one human gets on.

Hmm. That gives me an idea.

Maybe we don't need that stakeout after all.

9
How to Talk Human

Connor's scent disappeared in the middle of the street. That might have meant he got into a car. But he could have gotten into something else.

He could have gotten into a bus!

"We need to find out where that bus goes," I tell Mom. Finding out where that bus goes could be the key to finding Connor.

I give my leash a good tug. I'm

surprised when it flies out of Mom's hand. But I don't give her a chance to grab the leash back.

"Buddy!" Mom screams.

I hear her running behind me, but I need to get to that bus. I need to get there before the door closes and the bus drives away.

I feel a sharp jerk on my collar, and my whole body flies backwards. I fall to the ground with a thump.

"Caught you," Mom says. Her foot is firmly planted on top of my leash.

You sure did. Ow! My neck hurts.

The bus driver smiles as Mom picks up my leash. "Looks like your dog wants to ride the bus."

Mom gives the bus driver a half-hearted smile, then says to me, "Come on, Buddy. Dogs aren't allowed on buses."

"What? Why not?"

The door to the bus closes, and the bus pulls away.

"Let's go home," Mom says.

"But…but…how are we going to find out where that bus goes if we go home?" I ask. "If we don't find out where that bus goes we may never find Connor."

"You are so dumb," says a familiar voice behind me.

Huh?

I turn, and Cat with No Name slinks out between the bushes. "It says where the bus is going at the top of the window," he informs me.

"It does?" Unfortunately, the bus

is already gone, so I can't see where it's going. And even if I could see, I probably wouldn't be able to read the words. The only words I know how to read are: **P-o-U-N-D**, King, Kayla, vet, dog, cat, and food.

"Do you know where it's going?" I ask.

"Of course."

I hate that he can read and I can't.

"Will you tell me?" I ask. He probably won't.

But sometimes cats will surprise you. "All the buses that stop here go to the Minneapolis airport," he says.

And airports have airplanes that fly to California.

Back at the house, Mom just keeps pacing back and forth in front of the living room window. Watching. Waiting for Connor to come back. Or maybe waiting for the police to come back with news about him.

The police are not going to find him. Not here in the neighborhood. And they don't know that they need to go to the airport to look for him.

How do I get Mom to understand that we need to go to the airport?

I wonder if there is something in the house I can use to make her understand? I don't see anything in the living room, so I go to the kitchen. There are several bits of scrambled egg on the floor. I don't think these will help Mom understand anything, so I gobble them up. I LOVE scrambled eggs. They're my favorite food!

Then I head for Connor's room.

Hmm. The shirt that Connor wore while he slept is on the floor. I sniff. His scent is stronger here than anywhere else in the room. And there are airplanes all over the shirt. It's the perfect clue!

I grab the shirt in my mouth and bring it back to Mom.

She looks at it, but doesn't say anything.

I go back to Connor's room and look for something else to bring to Mom.

There's a toy airplane sticking out of a box. I grab that and race back to the living room.

Mom lets out another one of those big breaths of air. "Please don't drag things all over the house, Buddy," she says. She takes the airplane from me and drops it onto the couch next to Connor's shirt.

I trot back to Connor's room. What else can I show her?

There is a picture next to Connor's bed. It's a picture of him, Mom, and some man I've never met. They're all sitting on a front porch smiling. Is that Connor's dad?

I grab the picture, but the glass is heavy and slippery. It's hard to hold in my mouth. I have to balance it just so...there! Got it. I bring it to Mom.

"Buddy!" She sets the picture next to the airplane and the shirt.

She's getting mad now. But I
don't know what else to do. I don't
know how else to tell her what I
know.

All of a sudden she picks up the
airplane. She turns it around in her
hand. Her entire body freezes.

"I know Connor is unhappy about
moving to Minnesota. I wonder if
he's trying to find a way to go back
to California?"

"Yes!" I wag my tail.

"Maybe I should call the airport,"
she says, and she reaches for her cell
phone.

10
At the Top of the Moving Stairs

It's a long ride to the airport. Mom doesn't talk to me at all along the way. She just clenches the steering wheel and drives.

But it's okay because I am IN THE CAR! I'm going to the airport to get Connor, too.

I didn't ask if I could come. I just followed Mom out to the car. She didn't notice me until she opened the door and I squeezed in ahead of her.

"Buddy!" she said. "You can't come to the airport."

I went all the way over to the window, sat down, and pretended I didn't understand. Why not? That's what humans do to us.

Then something surprising happened. Mom said, "I've seen dogs in airports before. If I'm going to bring you to school, I need to know that you can behave in public. Plus, I bet Connor will be happy to see you."

And she let me stay in the car.

I can tell we're getting close to the airport now. I smell airplanes. I hear airplanes. And I *feel* airplanes. I have never been so close to a real airplane before. I didn't know that the whole earth shakes when they're around. Now that I've smelled and seen them up close, I don't think I like them very much.

Mom follows the road down below the ground and parks. It's dark here, and there are more cars than I have ever seen in one place before. It smells like poison, but I know it's only gasoline from all the cars.

Mom acts like she knows where we're going, so I let her take the lead. I follow her all the way to a big building. When we get there, the doors open right up for us. Like the building is expecting us.

It's very bright inside. And there are a lot of humans rushing around. Most of them are dragging suitcases

on wheels. I want to chase the suitcases, but I don't.

We need to find Connor. I don't
know how we're going to find him in
such a big place. I sniff and sniff, but
I don't smell him at all.

I do smell pizza, though. Over
there, under that chair. Mmm.
Pepperoni pizza. I grab it as we walk
by. I LOVE pepperoni pizza. It's my
favorite food!

Mom heads for the stairs. But
these are very strange stairs. They
rise up out of the floor. And they
move. So if you step on them you can
just stand there. You don't have to
climb them. They keep moving up,
up, up until they disappear into the
floor again at the very top.

I'm not sure I want to go on them. What if I disappear into the floor too?

But Mom doesn't give me a choice. "Come on, Buddy," she says, giving my leash a tug. And before I know it, I am on the strange moving stairway.

Help me! I don't want to be sucked into the floor...I don't want to die...

But all you have to do is step off the moving stairs when you get to the top. No problem.

Mom and I keep walking. We turn a corner and walk some more.

My nose twitches. Bacon... eggs...toothpaste...dirt...There are other smells mixed with the bacon, eggs, toothpaste, and dirt. I smell a bus and potato chips and turkey, too. But I'm sure all of it mixed together is Connor.

We come to a window where there's a lady sitting at a computer in another room. Connor is in there with her. The lady gets up and opens a door. Connor rushes toward us.

"Oh, Connor!" Mom cries, hugging him really, really tight.

"Stop, you're squishing me," Connor says. But he's hugging her back. I can tell he's just as happy to see her as she is to see him.

I lick both their arms and Connor's face. I am happy that they are happy.

And I'm *so* happy that this mystery is solved.

Mom and Connor talk for a while about human stuff like how you should never run away. And how you should never get on a bus without telling someone. And how scared Mom was when Connor didn't come back with me this morning. And how much Connor misses his dad and his friends.

To tell the truth, I don't pay much attention. Now that the Case of the Lost Boy is solved, it's time for me to start thinking about the Case of the Missing Family again.

I still want to solve that case. But now I'm a little bit worried about what's going to happen when I do solve it.

Who will I live with?

I always thought I'd go back to Kayla and her mom and dad. They

are my people.

But what about Connor and his mom? They *need* a dog. Mom needs a dog she can take to school. That's not something any dog can do.

And Connor needs a dog to be his friend. His *buddy*.

Plus they picked me at the P-o-U-N-D. They weren't supposed to. Humans don't pick dogs; dogs pick humans. But they picked me, anyway. Because they *wanted* me. How do you leave people who want you so much?

Here's the question:

Is it possible for a dog to have more than one family?

I don't know. I guess I'll have to find my other family before I can answer that question.

"Ready to go home?" Mom asks.

Connor nods.

As we walk back to the car, he reaches into his pocket and pulls out part of a smashed turkey sandwich. He tears it in half and hands one half to me.

Oh, boy! I LOVE turkey sandwiches.

They're my favorite food!

Praise for The Buddy Files